A catalogue record for this book is available from the British Library

This version published by Ladybird Books Ltd
27 Wrights Lane London W8 5TZ
A Penguin Company
© LADYBIRD BOOKS LTD MCMXCIX
1 3 5 7 9 10 8 6 4 2
LADYBIRD and the device of a Ladybird are trademarks of Ladybird Books Ltd

Hippity Hop, It's Baby Bop!™

written by Deborah Wormser
illustrated by June Valentine-Ruppe

Ladybird

Here's Baby Bop, Baby Boppity-Bop.

She jumps in the air with a hippity-hop.

She rides on her horse...

...with a rockety-rock.

She puts on her shoes and her sockety-socks.

She puts on her hat with a
ratta-tat-tat,

And pats the cat with a
patty-pat-pat.

She plays outside on her trikety-trike

With her brother BJ who she likety-likes.

At the make-believe store, with her carty-cart-cart,

She's ready for the fun to starty-start-start.

She brings out her dolls, and they all wait to see

What Baby Boppity-Bop is making for tea.

She stirs the tea with a spoony-spoon-spoon

While her friend Barney plays a
tuney-tune-tune.

Now she's so tired she could
droppity-drop.

It must be time to stoppity-stop.

She brushes her teeth…

...with a brushy-brush-brush,

And reads bedtime stories,

Night is hushy-hush-hush.

Good night, sleep tight, Baby Boppity-Bop.